The stories in this collection were first published individually by
Andersen Press Ltd., 20 Vauxhall Bridge Road, London SW1V 2SA, Great Britain as

Mucky Pup © 1997 Ken Brown
Lucky Mucky Pup © 1999 Ken Brown
Monster Mucky Pup © 2005 Ken Brown

This collection © 2005 Andersen Press Ltd., London
This edition published specially for Barnes and Noble, Inc 2005 by Andersen Press Ltd

Colour separated in Switzerland by Photolitho AG, Zürich
Printed and bound by Tien Wah Press, Singapore

4 6 8 10 9 7 5 3

ISBN 0-7607-9596-7

visit us at www.andersenpress.co.uk

The Adventures of
LUCKY PUP

Written and illustrated by
Ken Brown

Andersen Press
London

Contents

LUCKY PUP

Lucky Pup was having a wonderful time. He emptied the
wastepaper basket, he cleaned out the bucket that held
the fireplace ashes,

he rearranged the tablecloth and shook the cushions – what fun.

The farmer's wife didn't
think it was such fun.
"Oh you messy little pup,"
she cried. "Out you go."

But Lucky Pup wanted to play.
He saw the rooster.
"Will you play with me?" he asked.
"Cockadoodledon't be stupid," crowed the rooster.
"I'm a beautiful rooster – you're just a messy little pup."

Pup saw the duckling.

"Will you play with me?" he asked.

"You must be quack, quack, quackers," quacked the duckling.

"I'm a fluffy duckling – you're just a messy little pup."

Pup saw the cat.
"Will you play with me?" he asked.
"How perrrfectly ridiculous," purred the cat.
"I'm a handsome cat – you're just a messy little pup."

Pup saw the horse.
"Will you play with me please, please?"
"Nay, nay," neighed the horse.
"I'm a magnificent horse – you're just a messy little pup."

Pup was sad. Who would play with him?
Perhaps they were right after all – he was too messy.
He wandered outside into the yard.

Suddenly a snout appeared through the bars of the gate.
"Hello," said the piglet. "Will you play with me?"
"No," said Pup. "I'm just a messy little pup."
"But I'm just a messy little pig," said the piglet. "Let's play in the messy mud!"

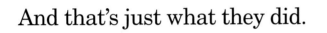

And that's just what they did.

Until ...

"Pup, Lucky Pup!" called the farmer's wife, "Bathtime!"
But Lucky Pup didn't need a bath.

He was a good, clean, clever pup,
and he settled down by the fire
to dream about playing with
his messy little piglet
friend tomorrow.

For Hogan and Tamara

LUCKY PUP
IN TROUBLE AGAIN

Lucky Pup was snoozing in the sun
when a bee buzzed by.

He snapped at it.

He jumped at it.

CRASH

bzzz

He pounced at it.

SMASH

bzzz

But the bee buzzed on . . .

So Lucky Pup chased it –
into the vegetable garden . . .

bzzz

WHOOPS

and into the farmyard.

"Come on, Pig!" he called.
"Come and chase this bee with me!"

bzzz

WHOOOSH

They chased it through the barn . . .

CLUCK!

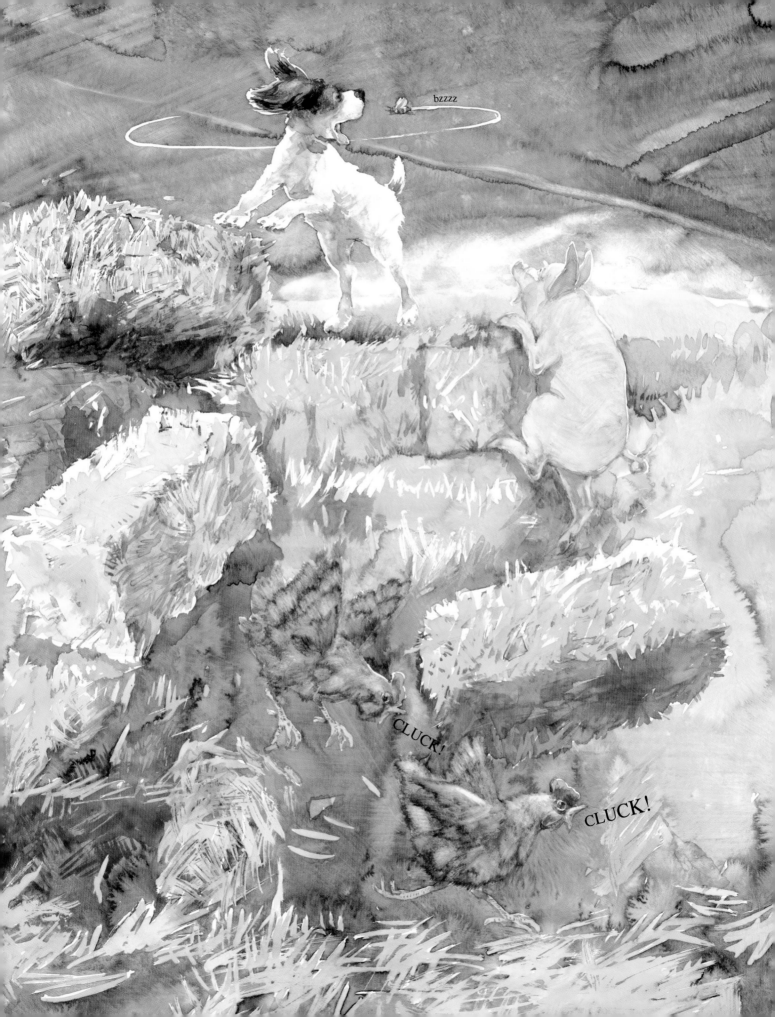

past the shed and around the pond

bzzz

and into the meadow.

bzzzzzzzzzzzzzzzzzzzzZZZZZZZZZZ

"Where's that bee gone now?"
panted Lucky pup.
"To fetch his friends," gasped Pig. "Look!"
Lucky Pup looked and . . . Uh-oh!

"RUUUUUUN!"

And how they ran! Out of the meadow . . .

bzzzzzzzzzzzzzzzzzzzzzzzzzzz

past the shed and across
the pond . . .

SPLASH

DASH

bzzzzzzzzzzzzzzzzz

bzzzzzzzzzzzzzzzzzzzzzzzz

back to the barn

and under the hay,

bzzzzzzzzzzzzzzzzzzz

down the hill and into . . .

bzzzzzzzzz

SPLAT!

bzzzzzzzzz

. . . the farmyard,

into the garden and under the wash,
safe and sound!
  But . . .

"Lucky Pup! What have you been doing?"
cried the farmer's wife.

"Poor Lucky Pup. *He's* not to blame," said the children.
"He was being chased by that swarm of bees."

"Well, he's lucky they didn't catch him," said their mom.
"Come on, Lucky Pup,
let's clean you up."

bzzzzzzzzzzzzzzz

So, instead of getting a scolding, Lucky Pup had a bath under the garden hose. And that was *much* more fun.

MONSTER
LUCKY PUP

Lucky Pup had chased things all morning.
He'd chased a fly . . .

He'd chased the leaves . . .

He'd even chased his tail . . .

But now he was bored with chasing things.
Then he saw that the shed door was open.
"That looks more fun," thought Lucky Pup . . .

And indeed it was . . .

. . . but it would be even more fun with two.
So Lucky Pup set off to find his friend, Pig, to join in.

"Hello, Hen," said Lucky Pup. "Have you seen Pig?"
But Hen just shrieked and flew away!
"She's very unfriendly," thought Lucky Pup,
puzzled. "How strange!"

"Hello, Cat," said Lucky Pup. "Have you seen Pig?" But Cat just yowled and fled across the farmyard!
"And *she's* even more unfriendly than usual," thought Lucky Pup.

"Hello, Duck," said Lucky Pup. "Have you seen Pig?"
But Duck just leapt off her nest into the water, quacking loudly!
"Now that really is odd," thought Lucky Pup.

Quack! Quack!

Quack!

Quack!

Quack!

Quack!

Quack!

"Hello, Donkey," said Lucky Pup. "Have you seen Pig?"
But Donkey brayed in a panic, kicked up his heels
and galloped away across the field.
"What is *wrong* with everybody?"
thought Lucky Pup.

HEEEE-
Haaaww!

HEEEE-
Haaaww!

"Hello, Goat," called Lucky Pup. "Have you seen . . . ?"

But before he could finish, Goat lowered his head and charged across the orchard towards him. This time it was Lucky Pup's turn to run, and run he did – as fast as he could, across the field and through the hedge to safety!

As he was catching his breath, he heard a familiar voice:
"Hello, Lucky Pup!"

"PIG!" gasped Lucky Pup. "Am I glad to see you! All the animals have gone mad. They've all run away from me except Goat, and he chased me across the orchard!"

"I'm not surprised," said Pig. "Just come over here,
and look at yourself in the stream!"
Lucky Pup looked. He got such a fright . . .

. . . that he grabbed hold of Pig!

They lost their balance and splashed into the stream . . .

. . . and that really was fun!

"LUCKY PUP, LUCKY PUP!"
"Uh-oh," said Pig. "They're calling you. Time to go!"

"Oh, what a mess!" they heard
the farmer's wife exclaim . . .

"Well you can't blame Lucky Pup
this time," said the children.
"Just look how clean he is!
Come on, Lucky Pup,
say goodbye to Pig.
It's time for lunch!"